This igloo book belongs to:

....

Contents

igloobooks

Published in 2015
by Igloo Books Ltd
Cottage Farm
Sywell
NN6 0BJ
www.igloobooks.com

LEO002 0515
4 6 8 10 9 7 5 3
ISBN 978-1-78197-052-2

Printed and manufactured in China

Illustrated by Shelagh McNicholas
Written by Jenny Simmons

Stories for

Year Old Girls

igloobooks

The Sparkly Shoes

Fairy Twinkle was trying out her new wand. She wanted a pair of sparkly shoes, just like her friend, Cherrybud. **Zing!** She swished her wand, but a pair of old, blue boots appeared.

Twinkle tried again. This time, she waved her wand a bit harder. There was a cloud of sparkles. When Twinkle looked down, she was wearing a pair of funny, yellow flippers.

"I must be doing it wrong," said Twinkle. "Maybe I need some magic words." She thought very hard and then said, "I want lovely shoes that shine. Bring me shoes that are all mine."

Suddenly, a pair of orange shoes appeared, then a blue pair, then a white pair and a purple pair, too. More shoes appeared every minute. "Help!" cried Twinkle. "Make them stop!"

Cherrybud came to help. She waved her wand and all of the shoes disappeared. "You just need to say the right words," said Cherrybud.

"Bring to Twinkle shoes that shimmer.
One red pair that glitter and glimmer."

Twinkle said the magic words and a pair of sparkly, red shoes appeared. "Thank you, Cherrybud," she said, with a big smile . The two fairies played happily in their sparkly shoes and Twinkle was so pleased to have such a wonderful best friend.

Flora at the Fair

Flora had never been to the Fairy Funfair before. She wasn't sure that she liked the loud music, or the flashing lights. **Whoosh**! went a big, twirly ride that span round and round.

Everything seemed so big and there were lots of loud noises.
"I'm scared," said Flora. She held on to her mother's hand tightly.
"Don't worry," said Mum. "The fair is lots of fun."

Mum bought Flora an enormous stick of delicious, pink, sticky candyfloss. "It's yummy," said Flora. All around them, big rides **whizzed** and **whooshed**. Then, Flora spotted a little, blue train. "I want to go on that," she said.

The blue train chugged as it went up and down the curvy track. "This isn't scary at all!" said Flora. **Toot**, **toot**! went the little, blue train. Flora thought that maybe the fair wasn't so bad after all.

Next, Flora played the hook-a-duck game. She stretched as far as she could and suddenly, she hooked a yellow duck with the number 1 on it. "You've won a giant teddy!" cried Mum. "Well done, Flora."

Flora took her giant teddy on the teacup ride. She giggled happily as they swirled and whirled round and round. "I'm not scared anymore," said Flora. "I think being at the fair is lots of fun."

Dancing Charlotte

Princess Charlotte loved to dance, but it was no fun on her own. "Please dance with me," she begged her dad. So, the king tried to waltz with Charlotte, but he kept treading on her toes.

"I'll dance with you," said the queen. "I used to love twirling at the annual royal ball!" She took Charlotte's hands and whirled her round and round, until the queen started to feel very dizzy.

Charlotte tried some ballet with the butler and tap-danced with the royal cook. She twirled and whirled with everyone in the palace and soon they had to sit down, because they were all exhausted!

"I want to keep dancing," said Charlotte, but everyone was too tired. Charlotte was very disappointed. "What you need is a party," said the queen, "with lots of music and dancing."

So, the king and queen invited all of Princess Charlotte's friends to a royal music party. The music started and everyone bopped, bounced and boogied to the beat. It was so much fun.

Charlotte loved her special music party. "Thank you, Mum and Dad," she said. "Dancing with grown-ups in the palace was fun, but dancing with all of my best friends is much better!"

The Scary Storm

Sparkle was picking daisies in the meadow when suddenly, a huge, dark storm cloud appeared. "Oh, no," squeaked Sparkle, feeling scared. Just then, a flash of lightning streaked across the sky.

The frightened fairy flitted into the woods to hide. She flew as fast as she could, as thunder **boomed** and **rumbled** above the treetops. Soon, Sparkle's wings were worn out and she had to stop to rest.

Plop! A raindrop landed on Sparkle's head. "I'm scared and I'm lost," she said, sadly. "Now I'm getting all wet, too." Sparkle was about to cry when she saw two little fairies carrying purple petal umbrellas.

"Hello. We're Splish and Splash, the storm fairies," they said.
"Don't be frightened. Storms are lots of fun."
Splish and Splash showed Sparkle how to jump between puddles
and how to dance so that the water splashed everywhere.

Splish turned her petal umbrella upside down and the three friends climbed inside. They spent all afternoon bobbing along the Rainbow River. Soon, the sun was shining brightly again. "It's time for us to go," said the storm fairies.

Sparkle's new friends took her back to the meadow and waved goodbye as they fluttered away. "I'll look out for you next time it thunders," said Sparkle. "I'll never be scared of storms again."

The Pink Party

Princess Rosy loved pink. She wore pink clothes, ate pink sweets and even had a pretty pink poodle as a pet. So, on her birthday, Rosy really wanted everything at her party to be pink.

The queen gave Rosy a bright orange and red dress to wear to the party. "Thank you," said the princess. She thought the dress was very pretty, but there was just one problem. It wasn't pink!

Then, the royal cook came in carrying a giant green and yellow birthday cake. Rosy thought it looked lovely and very yummy, but it still wasn't pink, so she was very disappointed.

When her friends arrived, Rosy thanked them for the presents that they gave her, even though none of them were pink. The queen saw that the princess was sad and suddenly realised what was wrong.

The queen asked the cook to whip up some pink cupcakes. Then, she quickly put up lots and lots of pink decorations. Finally, she found some pink ribbons and tied them into bows to add to Rosy's dress.

"I thought you might want a change from pink," said the queen. "Now I can see that you like it more than ever!" Rosy gave her mum a giant hug. Her party was perfectly pink after all.

The Magical Unicorn

My unicorn is the best. Together, we fly high above the sparkly, candyfloss clouds. We say hello to the little birds that we see, as we **whoosh** past the glittery rainbows in the Fairyland sky.

We stop at the Lemonade River for a yummy picnic with my best fairy friends. There are caramel cupcakes and strawberry pastries for everybody to eat. My unicorn sometimes gets a treat, too!

Sometimes, we fly to the Lollipop Wood. We jump and twirl around the lollipop trees, while our unicorns munch on the tasty grass. My unicorn is always friendly and kind to everyone.

When the bright moon and stars appear in the sky, my unicorn flies me home. "Goodnight," I say to my unicorn, giving him a hug. "Thank you for being the best unicorn ever."

The Best Friend Necklace

Princess Zara and Princess Anna were best friends. One day, when they were playing dressing-up, Zara found a beautiful necklace. "This will go perfectly with my purple shoes," said Anna, snatching it from Zara's hand.

"It would look better with my orange ones," said Zara, crossly pulling the necklace back. The princesses tugged it back and forth between them, until suddenly, the lovely necklace **snapped** in half.

Just then, Anna's mum called, saying it was time for Anna to go home. Zara sadly watched her best friend leave, still holding one half of the necklace. She had never fought with Anna before.

The queen saw how sad Princess Zara was and asked her what had happened. Zara told the queen all about the broken necklace. "I've got an idea," said the queen. "What if you made Princess Anna a special present?"

The next day, Princess Zara and the queen went to visit Princess Anna. "I'm sorry for fighting with you," said Zara. She handed Anna a new heart necklace, made from half of the necklace they had snapped in two.

"I made you a present, too," giggled Anna. She gave Zara a necklace made from the other broken half! It had a shiny star pendant on it. The two princesses hugged. They knew they were going to be best friends forever.

The Painting Princesses

It was a rainy day, so Princess Amelia and Princess Harriet got out their paintbrushes and paint pots. "Let's paint a picture of daddy," they said. "Try not to make a mess," said the queen.

Amelia sploshed her paintbrush in the pink pot and drew a small circle. Harriet splished her brush in the purple pot and drew a big circle. **Splish**, **splash**, they went, as they splodged bright paint all over the page.

Splodge, **splat**! Harriet painted a red nose. "I will paint him some arms and legs," said Amelia. She stuck her fingers in a pot of orange paint and splatted it onto the paper.

The princesses splatted and splashed until they were covered in paint. Just then, the king came in. "What an interesting picture you've painted," he said. "Is it a monster?"

Princess Harriet and Princess Amelia both giggled.
"It's a picture of you, Daddy," they said.
"It can go in the royal gallery," said the king, laughing, "but first, you two had better have a bath!"